Dear Parent:
Your child's love of reading starts here!

Every child learns to read in a different way and at his or her own speed. Some go back and forth between reading levels and read favorite books again and again. Others read through each level in order. You can help your young reader improve and become more confident by encouraging his or her own interests and abilities. From books your child reads with you to the first books he or she reads alone, there are I Can Read Books for every stage of reading:

SHARED READING
Basic language, word repetition, and whimsical illustrations, ideal for sharing with your emergent reader

BEGINNING READING
Short sentences, familiar words, and simple concepts for children eager to read on their own

READING WITH HELP
Engaging stories, longer sentences, and language play for developing readers

READING ALONE
Complex plots, challenging vocabulary, and high-interest topics for the independent reader

ADVANCED READING
Short paragraphs, chapters, and exciting themes for the perfect bridge to chapter books

I Can Read Books have introduced children to the joy of reading since 1957. Featuring award-winning authors and illustrators and a fabulous cast of beloved characters, I Can Read Books set the standard for beginning readers.

A lifetime of discovery begins with the magical words "I Can Read!"

Visit www.icanread.com for information
on enriching your child's reading experience.

For H.B.
—D.C.

For Doreen
—H.B.

I Can Read Book® is a trademark of HarperCollins Publishers.

Text copyright © 2013 by Doreen Cronin. Illustrations copyright © 2013 by Harry Bliss. All rights reserved. Manufactured in China. No part of this book may be used or reproduced in any manner whatsoever without written permission except in the case of brief quotations embodied in critical articles and reviews. For information address HarperCollins Children's Books, a division of HarperCollins Publishers, 10 East 53rd Street, New York, NY 10022.
www.icanread.com
Library of Congress catalog card number: 2012937018
ISBN 978-0-06-208705-8 (trade bdg.)—ISBN 978-0-06-208704-1 (pbk.)

Typography by John Sazaklis

13 14 15 16 17   SCP   10 9 8 7 6 5 4 3 2 1   ❖   First Edition

I Can Read!™

BEGINNING READING 1

DIARY OF A WORM

Teacher's Pet

Based on the creation of
Doreen Cronin and Harry Bliss
by Lori Haskins Houran
pictures by John Nez

HARPER
An Imprint of HarperCollinsPublishers

October 3

Today is Thursday.

It is almost the weekend!

I love weekends.

I get to hang out

with Spider and Fly.

I wish we went to the same school.

But I guess that wouldn't work.

I can't see Fly in Squirming class.

And I already know

Spider can't dig.

October 4

We had a sub at school today.

Mrs. Mulch took the day off

for her birthday.

I didn't know teachers had days off.

Or birthdays.

The sub said, "Why don't you have a party for Mrs. Mulch on Monday?"

After lunch, everyone talked about
what they were going to give
Mrs. Mulch at the party.
A fuzzy mold pillow.
An eggshell candy dish.

Me?

I had tons of ideas.

October 5

What to Give Mrs. Mulch

1. Dung ball paperweight

2. Silk slippers

3. Trash Splash perfume

4. Gum wrapper scarf

1. Dung ball paperweight
Fly's idea—but dung is not for everyone.

2. Silk slippers
From Spider. He forgot that worms don't have feet!

3. Trash Splash perfume
My sister's dumb idea. Do teachers even wear perfume?

4. Gum wrapper scarf
From my dad.

13

The gum wrapper idea isn't bad.

Except my dad just ate

the last gum wrapper.

Argh! I have to think of something.

Mrs. Mulch is the best teacher

I have ever had!

October 6

I woke up worried.

One more day until the party

and I was still stumped.

To take my mind off my troubles,

Spider and Fly picked me up

to go kite-flying.

Even that didn't cheer me up.

"Thanks for trying, guys,"

I said glumly.

Just then, Fly spotted something
with one of her zillion eyes.
"Hey, what's that?" she said.

It was an apple.
A big, red,
shiny one.

Teachers love apples!

But wait a second.

Was it rotten?

Spider took me down to check.

I poked the apple.

SQUISH.

It was rotten all right.

YES! HOORAY!

The perfect present at last!

Now I just had to get it

to my school.

I pushed.

Spider pulled.

Fly cheered.

It took forever,
but we made it.

October 7

Party day!

I was feeling good.

Then I heard someone say,

"I found a great card for my gift.

Mrs. Mulch will love it."

CARD?

Uh-oh.

Lucky for me,

I hadn't eaten breakfast yet.

I finished just in time.

Mrs. Mulch was thrilled.

I gave her three things in one:

a birthday gift,

a birthday card,

and a birthday surprise!

Present for my teacher